CONTENTS

A LITTLE SCARY

"Welcome to Hitchcock's House of Wax!" Dad exclaimed.

The old, scary building on the corner had been redone. It still looked old and scary. Vincent was not impressed.

"It looks . . . interesting," Vincent said.

Vincent was nervous. Those lifelike wax statues creeped him out. But he was determined to do this. He wanted to try new things, even if they were hard.

"It's awesome!" said his dad. "Let's go!"

Vincent looked around the main floor. He saw film stars, sports stars and other famous figures. He liked films and sport.

Maybe this isn't so bad, he thought.

That was when he saw the sign.

A sign he did NOT want to see.

"What's in there?" Vincent asked.

"Only one way to find out," said his dad.

Just when I thought this would be fun, Vincent thought.

Dad pulled back the heavy red curtain. Vincent nearly jumped out of his skin.

"*AAAAH!*" he screamed.

There were monsters everywhere!

"It's the Hall of Horrors! I was hoping they would have this," said Dad. "It's full of monsters and more!"

This was exactly what Vincent was scared of. He was fine with the film and sports stars, and other famous figures in wax form. But monsters? No, thank you!

"Let's take a closer look," his dad said, smiling.

Vincent tried to smile. He took a deep breath. He reminded himself that he could do hard things. Then he followed his dad into the eerie room.

His dad went to look at a werewolf. Vincent stared at a spooky vampire. The vampire stared back.

Suddenly, it moved.

CHAPTER TWO
A LOT SCARY

Vincent ran screaming. He had to find his dad.

"You have to see this!" the boy cried. "Hurry up!"

When they returned, the vampire was gone.

"Very clever," said Dad. "It's the Invisible Man!"

Vincent couldn't even reply. He knew there had been a vampire there before. What was going on?

"Dad, I'm serious," said Vincent.

He moved closer to the empty
space.

"There was a vampire standing
here, and he looked like . . . THAT!"
Vincent screamed.

The vampire reappeared behind the boy. With him were a werewolf and a witch.

Vincent hid behind his father.

"They've really upgraded this place," said Dad. "The statues don't normally move around."

Vincent felt a twinge of terror.

"I think this place is haunted. Time to go!" Vincent yelled.

"Just relax, buddy," his dad said. "They aren't real."

Vincent was not convinced.

Suddenly, something emerged
from the shadows. The boy whirled
around.

"Swamp creature!" he screamed.

"*AHHHHH*!" his dad screamed.

The monster opened its mouth.

It had rows of sharp, scary teeth.

"Don't eat me!" yelled Vincent.

"Don't eat either of us!" his dad
yelled.

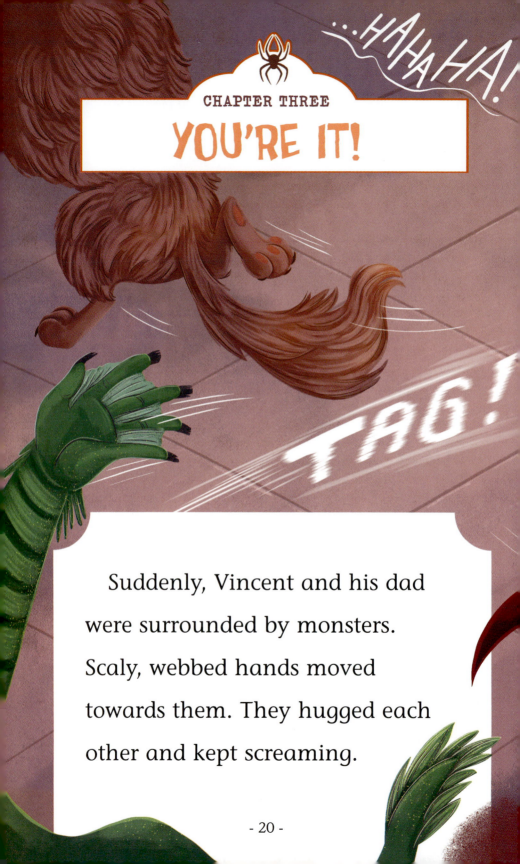

Suddenly, Vincent and his dad were surrounded by monsters. Scaly, webbed hands moved towards them. They hugged each other and kept screaming.

"TAG!" yelled the creature. "You're IT!"

Quick as a flash, the monsters ran away.

HEHEHE...

Vincent and his father stared at each other. They could hear the monsters giggling with glee.

"I think they just want to play tag," his dad said.

"What are you waiting for?" asked Vincent. "Let's get 'em!" The chase was on.

The new friends played until closing time. Vincent was happy he had overcome his fears and tried something new.

"Thanks so much," said the werewolf. "We get lonely."

"I expect people are afraid to visit us," added the witch.

"Don't worry," said Vincent.
"We know just where to come
to scare up some fun!"

AUTHOR

John Sazaklis is a *New York Times* bestselling author with almost 100 children's books under his utility belt! He has also illustrated Spider-Man books, created toys for *MAD* magazine and written for the BEN 10 animated series. John lives in New York, USA, with his superpowered wife and daughter.

ILLUSTRATOR

Patrycja Fabicka is an illustrator with a love for magic, nature, soft colours and storytelling. Creating cute and colourful illustrations is something that warms her heart – even during cold winter nights. She hopes that her artwork will inspire children, as she was once inspired by *The Snow Queen, Cinderella* and other fairy tales.

GLOSSARY

determined having a firm or fixed purpose

eerie strange and frightening

emerge come into view

nervous feeling worried

twinge sudden feeling

DISCUSSION QUESTIONS

1. Were you surprised by the twist in the story? Why or why not?

2. Why is it important to try new things?

3. How do you think the monsters felt at the beginning of the story? How do you think they felt at the end?

WRITING PROMPTS

1. Make a list of at least five people (or monsters) that you would want to see in a wax museum.

2. It's important to try new things, even if you are scared. Write about something new that you have tried.

3. Pretend you are one of the monsters in the story. Write a diary entry about your exciting day.

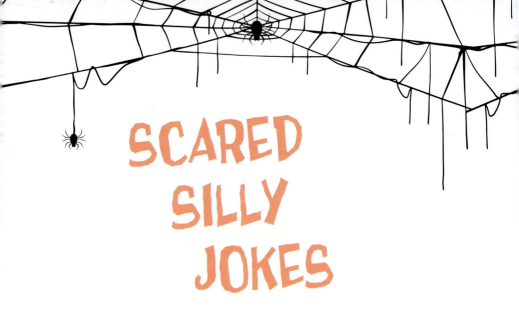

SCARED SILLY JOKES

What is a swamp monster's favourite treat?

marshmallows

Why is cricket a vampire's favourite sport?

because of all the bats

Why are vampires hard to get along with?

They can be a pain in the neck.

Why did the vampire go to school?

to learn the alphabat

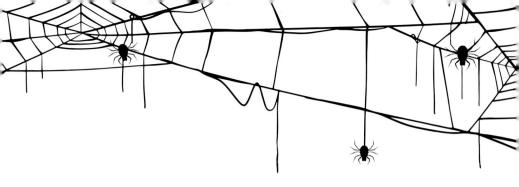

What do witches put in their hair?
scare spray

What do you call witches who live together?
broommates

What's a witch's favourite subject at school?
spelling

What do you get if you cross a witch with winter?
a cold spell

BOO BOOKS

Discover these just-right frights!

Only from Raintree

CONTENTS

CHAPTER ONE

'TIS THE SEASON

Anna Maria loved winter! She couldn't wait to play in the snow. Her twin sister, Eirini, did not feel the same way.

"It's the most wonderful time of the year!" Anna Maria sang.

SNOWBALL FRIGHT

by John Sazaklis

illustrated by Patrycja Fabicka

Raintree is an imprint of Capstone Global Library Limited, a company
incorporated in England and Wales having its registered office at
264 Banbury Road, Oxford, OX2 7DY – Registered company number:
6695582

www.raintree.co.uk
myorders@raintree.co.uk

Designed by Nathan Gassman
Original illustrations © Capstone Global Library Limited 2024
Originated by Capstone Global Library Ltd

978 1 3982 5470 1

British Library Cataloguing in Publication Data
A full catalogue record for this book is available from the
British Library.

Printed and bound in India

"No, it's not," replied Eirini. "I like my weather hot and sunny."

Anna Maria wished that her sister would cheer up.

"Do you want to build a snowman?" Anna Maria asked.

"Nope," Eirini said.

"You're such a grump," said Anna Maria. "You should be nice because Father Christmas is watching."

"That big, boring bozo isn't as cool as Krampus," Eirini said.

"Whatever. I'm going to build a snowman," Anna Maria said.

Eirini sat by the fireplace with her Krampus story. It was her favourite. She read it every year.

Krampus was a folktale about a big goat-man with horns that scared children at Christmas.

Suddenly, Eirini had a wicked idea.

"I'll help my sister build a snow monster instead of a snowman," she whispered.

She turned to a magic spell. Then she chanted:

"Krampus, Krampus, are you there? Give my sister a big old scare!"

The lights flickered. The fire roared. Eirini smiled.

Anna Maria was putting the finishing touches to her snowman when suddenly . . .

OooOOoooOOO!

The wind howled. The sky turned dark. Then two branch-arms grabbed Anna Maria.

"BOO!" yelled the snowman.

Anna Maria screamed. "You're alive!"

"And you're mine!" it shouted back.

CHAPTER TWO

CHILLIN' LIKE A VILLAIN

Anna Maria broke through the twig fingers. She sprinted towards the house.

"Oh, what fun it is to run!" said the snowman, chasing Anna Maria.

Eirini watched from the window while her sister was chased by a scary snow monster.

"'Twas the fright before Christmas!" she said with a laugh.

THUNK! THUNK! THUNK!

Anna Maria banged on the window.

"Help me! My snowman is alive!" she shouted.

"I know!" Eirini shouted back.

PLOP! PLOP! SMASH!

Snowballs crashed against the glass. Then they began to change. They now had freaky faces of their own!

Anna Maria screamed as they pushed her down.

"Yikes," Eirini said. "This spooky spell is out of control!"

CHAPTER THREE

NAUGHTY AND NICE

Eirini tried to reverse the curse,
but every spell in the book was
naughty. To save her sister, Eirini
needed to be nice.

"I'll fix this monster mess myself!"
she said.

Eirini bundled up and ran
outside.

Anna Maria was fighting the frozen foes.

"Hey, Frosty!" Eirini shouted. "Over here!"

She bashed the snowman with a big branch.

SMASH!

The monster began to grow bigger.
"Silly girl! Your wicked ways only
make me stronger!"
The sisters were in double trouble!

"I was just trying to help!" Eirini shouted.

"Teamwork only works with kindness," said Anna Maria. "You started this, but WE can finish it!"

She ran into the house. Eirini followed, and so did the snowman.

The sisters headed for the fireplace. Quick as a flash, they jumped out of the way.

The snow monster was blasted by the heat.

"I'M MELTING!" he yelled and fell forward into the flames.

FWOOOOM!

"We did it!" Eirini cheered. Then she hugged her sister. "I'm sorry for what I did. I promise to be nicer."

"I'm glad you were moved by the Christmas spirit, even if it was haunted," Anna Maria said.

"So, what's the first thing you want to do together?" Eirini asked.

"Tidy up before Mum and Dad find out," Anna Maria replied. "It will be *snow* much fun!"

Eirini was not amused.

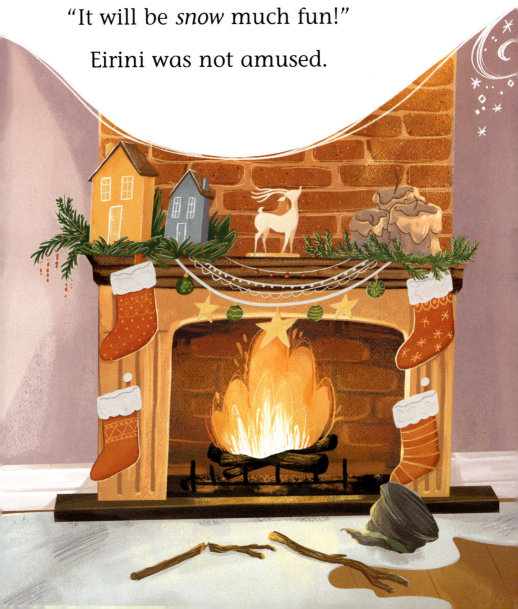

AUTHOR

John Sazaklis is a *New York Times* bestselling author with almost 100 children's books under his utility belt! He has also illustrated Spider-Man books, created toys for *MAD* magazine and written for the BEN 10 animated series. John lives in New York, USA, with his superpowered wife and daughter.

ILLUSTRATOR

Patrycja Fabicka is an illustrator with a love for magic, nature, soft colours and storytelling. Creating cute and colourful illustrations is something that warms her heart – even during cold winter nights. She hopes that her artwork will inspire children, as she was once inspired by *The Snow Queen, Cinderella* and other fairy tales.

GLOSSARY

bozo foolish person

foe enemy

reverse go the opposite way

spirit mood or feeling. Also another word for ghost.

wicked mean or unkind

DISCUSSION QUESTIONS

1. Eirini and her sister are complete opposites. Do you think it's easier or harder to be friends with someone who is your opposite?

2. Do you think Eirini was being funny or mean?

3. How do you think Anna Maria felt when her snowman came to life?

WRITING PROMPTS

1. Eirini and Anna Maria had to work together to solve the problem. Write about a time you used teamwork.

2. Everyone argues, especially siblings. Write about a time you were in an argument.

3. Make a list of at least three things you like to do during the winter.

SCARED SILLY JOKES!

What is a snowman's favourite summer drink?

iced tea

What do snowmen take when they get too hot?

a chill pill

What do snowmen use to do research?

the winternet

What do you call a fancy snowman dance?

a snowball

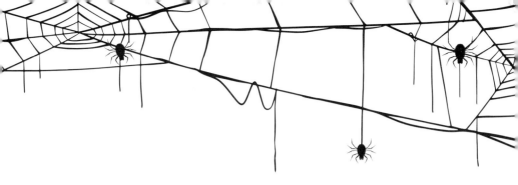

What did the police officer say to the snowman who was caught stealing?
Freeze!

What did the the snowman say to his best friend?
You're the coolest!

What did the snowman eat for breakfast?
Frosted Flakes

Where does a snowman keep his money?
a snowbank

BOO BOOKS

Discover these just-right frights!

Only from Raintree